BOOK ONE

Ashik Usman

Copyright © 2025 Ashik Usman
All rights reserved.
Set in Bree Serif, Merriweather and Ariel On Google Docs.
ISBN: 979-828-2586-56-5

DEDICATION

For I, A and Y. Always.

CONTENTS

Acknowledgments

Introduction   1

Part 1: The Shadow over Asfaran
Chapter 1: Whispers in the Souq   7
Chapter 2: The Imam's Vigil   12
Chapter 3: Secrets in the Veil   16
Chapter 4: Dust and Duty   26
Chapter 5: The Gathering Storm   32
Chapter 6: Council of War   39

Part 2: The Serpent's Coil
Chapter 7: The Road to Kufa's Whisper   41
Chapter 8: Trails of Corruption   46
Chapter 9: The Crusader Front   52
Chapter 10: Dungeon of the Djinn-Kings   56
Chapter 11: The Scholar's Revelation   65

Part 3: The Crescent Ascendant
Chapter 12: Siege of the Holy Place   69
Chapter 13: Infiltration and Assault   71
Chapter 14: The Heart of the Storm   76
Chapter 15: Dawn over the Horizon   81

About the Author

ACKNOWLEDGMENTS

This journey would not have been possible without the unwavering support of my family and friends. You have been my pillars of strength, my sounding boards, and my champions. Your encouragement has helped me weave words into the worlds I dreamed of.

I am forever indebted to the great minds who have shaped the fantasy landscapes that inspired me—J.R.R. Tolkien, C.S. Lewis, Guy Gavriel Kay, Raymond E. Feist, David and Leigh Eddings, Robert Jordan, and George R.R. Martin. Through your stories, I found my love for epic adventures, intricate world-building, and the magic of storytelling itself.

A special and heartfelt thanks to Steve Jackson and Ian Livingstone, whose Fighting Fantasy series first ignited my imagination and has stayed with me throughout my life. Your interactive storytelling opened doors to endless possibilities, teaching me that the reader could be the hero, that choices mattered, and that every path held adventure.

And finally, to the stories and traditions that have shaped me—my Islamic, Middle Eastern, and South Asian heritage. These rich histories, mythologies, and cultures are woven into the fabric of this book, a tribute to the legends that came before and the new journeys yet to be told.

Thank you all for walking this path with me.

INTRODUCTION

Welcome, Adventurer!

Welcome to *The Crescent & The Crypt,* an epic gamebook adventure set in a world of faith, steel, and terrifying shadows, inspired by the rich history and folklore of the Middle Ages!

In this book, YOU are the hero. Your journey will be perilous, filled with difficult choices and deadly challenges. Your fate is determined by the decisions you make and the outcome of dice rolls.

How to Play

You will need:

1. This book.
2. A pencil and paper to keep track of your stats and any items you find.
3. Two six-sided dice (2D6).

Your Hero

Before you begin, you must determine your hero's abilities. You have three core stats:

- ❖ **SKILL**: This represents your combat ability, agility, and general dexterity. The higher your Skill, the better you are at fighting and performing acrobatic feats.
- ❖ **STAMINA:** This is your life force, your health and endurance. When your Stamina reaches 0, your adventure ends!
- ❖ **LUCK:** Fate smiles upon some more than others. Luck can help you in difficult situations or avoid danger.

To determine your starting stats, roll the dice:
- ❖ Roll 1D6 and add 6 to get your starting **SKILL**. Record it.
- ❖ Roll 2D6 and add 12 to get your starting **STAMINA**. Record it.
- ❖ Roll 1D6 and add 6 to get your starting **LUCK**. Record it.

Example: If you roll a 4 for SKILL, your starting SKILL is 4 + 6 = 10. If you roll 3 and 5 for STAMINA, your starting STAMINA is 3 + 5 + 12 = 20. If you roll 2 for LUCK, your starting LUCK is 2 + 6 = 8.

THE CRESCENT AND THE CRYPT

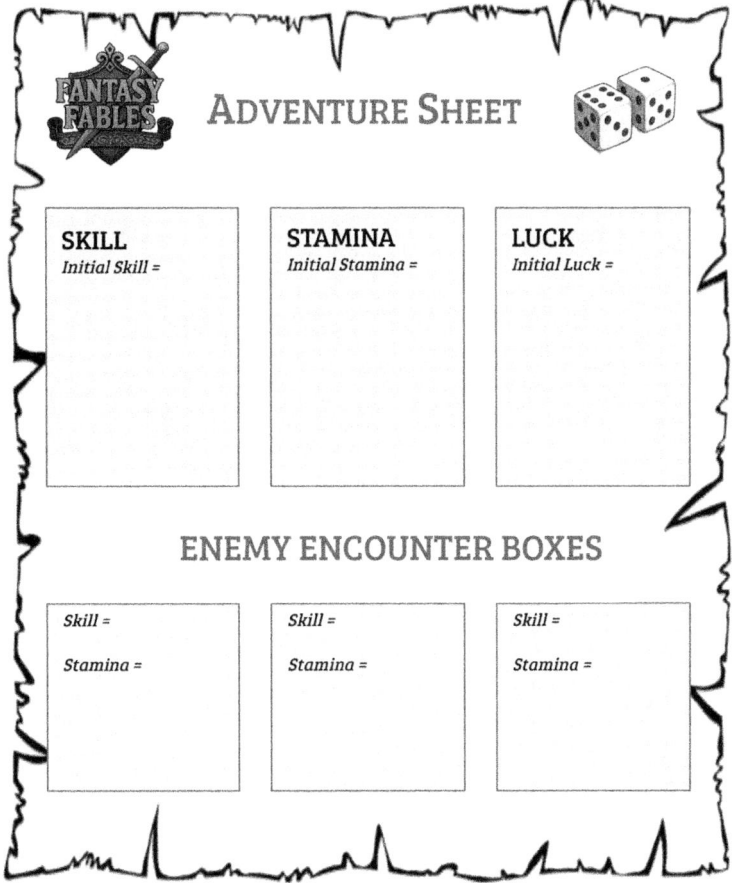

ADVENTURE SHEET

SKILL
Initial Skill =

STAMINA
Initial Stamina =

LUCK
Initial Luck =

ENEMY ENCOUNTER BOXES

Skill =

Stamina =

Skill =

Stamina =

Skill =

Stamina =

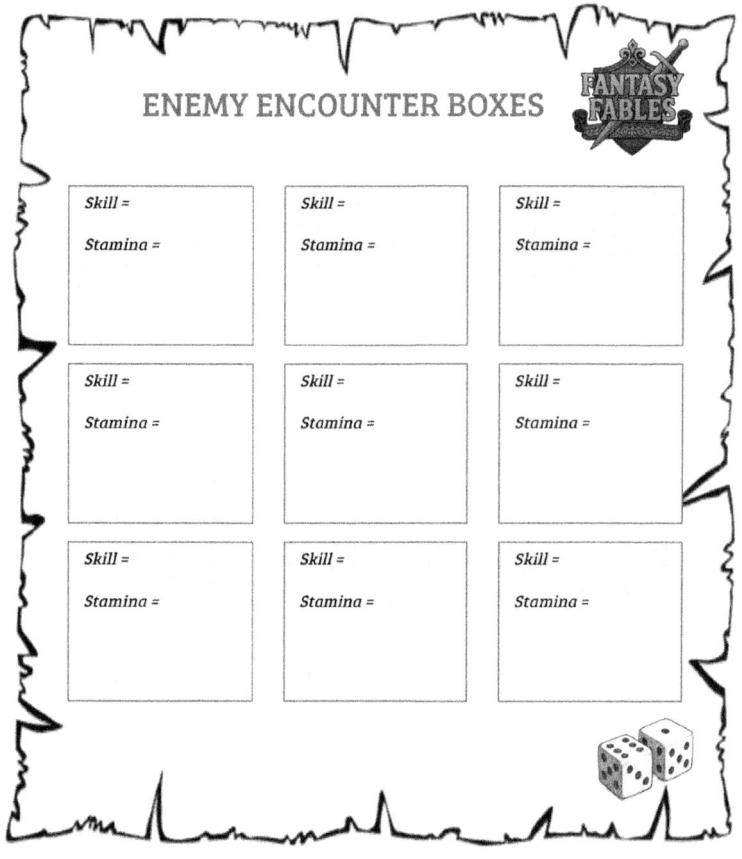

Testing Your Skill, Stamina, and Luck

- ❖ **Skill Tests:** You will often be instructed to Test your Skill. To do this, roll 2D6. If the result is less than or equal to your current SKILL score, you are **Successful**. If the result is greater than your current SKILL score, you are **Unsuccessful**.
- ❖ **Luck Tests:** You will sometimes be instructed to Test your Luck. To do this, roll 1D6. If the result is less than or equal to your current LUCK score, you are **Successful**. If the result is greater than your current LUCK score, you

are **Unsuccessful.** Sometimes, the test will specify an outcome based on whether the dice roll is Odd or Even when compared to your Luck (e.g., "If the roll is odd and <= Luck..."). Pay close attention to these instructions.

❖ **Spending Luck:** At certain points, usually before making a Skill Test or Luck Test (and sometimes during combat or to avoid a penalty), you may be given the option to spend a point of Luck. If you choose to spend Luck, you **immediately reduce your LUCK score by 1** and the test or situation's outcome is automatically treated as a Success, or the penalty is lessened/avoided as described. You cannot spend Luck if your current LUCK score is 0. You can only spend Luck when instructed that you have the option.

Combat

When you encounter an enemy, combat is resolved round by round. Each round:

1. **Roll for Attack:** You and the enemy will each roll 2D6 to determine who hits.
2. **Compare Attack Rolls:**
    - If your roll is higher than the enemy's SKILL, you hit them.
    - If the enemy's roll is higher than your SKILL, they hit you.
    - If the rolls are equal, neither hits.
3. **Deal Damage:** If you hit, roll 2D6 for damage and subtract that amount from the enemy's STAMINA. If the enemy hits you, roll 2D6 for damage and subtract that amount from your STAMINA.
4. **Continue:** Repeat steps 1-3 until either you or the enemy reaches 0 STAMINA.

If your STAMINA reaches 0 at any point, your adventure is over! It is GAME OVER and you will need to start again from the beginning.

Turning to Sections

At the end of most sections, you will be given instructions on where to turn. Follow these instructions carefully based on your choices or the outcome of dice rolls.

Now, sharpen your pencil and prepare yourself. Your journey begins!

PART 1: THE SHADOW OVER ASFARAN

CHAPTER 1: WHISPERS IN THE SOUQ

A bustling medieval souq street with arched market stalls. In the foreground, there are crates floating, with shadows forming unnatural shapes that look subtly wrong, and some merchants looking particularly fearful.

10

The air in the Great Souq of Asfaran is thick with the scent of cardamom, saffron, and roasting lamb. Merchants call out their wares beneath colourful awnings, and the murmur of a thousand conversations fills the space between the magnificent arched gateways and intricate tilework. You move through the crowd, a feeling of ease washing over you – this city, a jewel of the lands, feels safe and prosperous.

Suddenly, a sharp crack splinters the air, followed by a clatter and a cry of alarm. Ahead, near a spice merchant's stall, a wooden crate has seemingly exploded outwards, sending pungent peppers and cinnamon sticks scattering across the cobbled ground. People nearby recoil, muttering about bad luck or a particularly mischievous Jinn.

Do you:

- ❖ Investigate the collapsed stall and see if anything seems unnatural? Turn to **12**.
- ❖ Dismiss it as an accident and continue on your way? Turn to **15**.

12

You push through the murmuring crowd towards the ruined stall. The merchant is visibly shaken, pointing at the splintered wood. As you examine the debris, you notice the wood isn't just broken; it looks twisted and slightly charred, as if by an unseen force. A faint, unsettling whisper seems to slither into your ear from somewhere nearby – too low to make out words, but undeniably there, like dry leaves skittering across stone.

This feels like more than just mischievous Jinn.

Do you:

- ❖ Try to focus and discern the source and nature of the unsettling whisper? **Test your Skill.** If successful, turn to **18**. If unsuccessful, turn to **13**.
- ❖ Ignore the whisper for now and look instead for anyone acting suspiciously in the crowd around the collapsed stall? Turn to **14**.

13

You concentrate, trying to isolate the unsettling sound from the general clamor of the Souq. But the whisper is too faint, too elusive. It seems to fade away, lost in the noise of the marketplace. You cannot tell where it came from or what it was. You find nothing further here. The incident remains a mystery, adding to the growing unease you feel.

Turn to **19**.

14

Instead of focusing on the strange whisper, you scan the faces in the crowd, looking for anyone who seems out of place, too interested in the incident, or perhaps hurrying away. Most people are focused on the merchant and the mess, or simply trying to put distance between themselves and the odd event.
Then, at the edge of the throng, near an arched exit from the Souq, you spot a figure. They are moving quickly, perhaps too quickly, melting into the flow of people exiting the market. There's something about their posture or the unnatural fluidity of their movement that catches your eye.

Turn to **16**.

15

You decide the collapsed crate is likely just an unfortunate accident or, at worst, minor Jinn mischief that isn't worth your immediate attention. You continue deeper into the vibrant heart of the Souq. As you pass by other stalls, you overhear hushed conversations – a baker complaining about bread mysteriously turning to ash, a weaver finding impossible knots in their finest silk, children speaking of seeing distorted faces in reflective surfaces. The strange incidents aren't isolated. A feeling of unease begins to settle over the entire marketplace.

Turn to **19**.

16

You've spotted the figure hurrying away from the scene. They move with an unsettling grace, weaving through the crowd with unnatural ease. They are almost at the exit of the Souq.

Do you try to follow the figure without being noticed, hoping they lead you to answers? You'll need to be quick and subtle.

- ❖ Attempt to follow the figure secretly. **Test your Skill** or **Test your Luck** (your choice which one you want to use).
    - ➢ If Successful (on either test), turn to **20**.
    - ➢ If Unsuccessful (on either test), turn to **17**.
- ❖ Decide that following a potentially dangerous or supernatural figure is too risky in the crowded Souq for now. Turn to **19**.

17

You try to keep the figure in sight, slipping between people, but they are too fast, too adept at navigating the crowded space. They reach the Souq exit and vanish into the labyrinth of the city streets beyond before you can catch up or get a clear look at where they went. You've lost them.

Turn to **19**.

18

You close your eyes for a moment, focusing past the sounds of the market. The whisper coalesces, growing slightly stronger, though still distorted. It is not wind or the sounds of the crowd. It sounds like pained, hissing voices. And they are coming from below the ground, beneath the very cobblestones you stand on. The source feels ancient and filled with malice. This isn't Jinn mischief; this is something far darker, and it's lurking beneath the foundations of the city.

Turn to **19**.

19

Whether you investigated the stall, heard the whispers, saw the strange figure, or simply absorbed the general atmosphere of creeping unease, one thing is clear: something is deeply wrong in Asfaran. The strange occurrences are too frequent, too unnatural to be mere coincidence or petty spirits. It feels like a shadow is falling over the city, unseen but palpable. You realise you cannot ignore this. You need information, guidance, or allies.

You know two potential paths to understanding what is happening:

- ❖ Seek wisdom and knowledge from the respected religious scholars at the Grand Masjid. Their leader, Imam Tariq, is known for his deep learning, including studies of ancient and esoteric texts. Perhaps he knows of such portents. Turn to **22**
- ❖ Seek information from the less reputable, but often well-informed, inhabitants of the city's underbelly – merchants dealing in forbidden goods, those who know hidden ways, or hear whispers the common folk miss. Perhaps they know who or what is behind the strange events. Turn to **25**

Chapter 2: The Imam's Vigil

The interior of the study chamber of the Grand Mosque library. A wise-looking scholar is seated amongst stacks of ancient, ornate scrolls and texts. He is looking up from a scroll with a look of grave concern and deep contemplation.

22

You make your way through the city towards the Grand Masjid. As you approach, the unsettling atmosphere of the Souq gives way to a sense of peace and spiritual solace that seems to emanate from the holy place. The Masjid stands magnificent against the sky, its domes soaring, its minarets reaching like fingers towards the heavens. Inside, the air is cool and carries the faint scent of rosewater and incense. Worshippers pray in quiet devotion, and the outside world feels distant.

You inquire about Imam Tariq and are directed towards a quieter section of the Masjid, near a chamber filled with ancient texts and scrolls – a library of immense age and knowledge. You find the Imam here. He is an old man with a wise, kind face and eyes that hold the light of deep faith and learning. He is seated amongst stacks of fragile manuscripts, poring over a particularly large, illuminated scroll. He seems deeply engrossed, a look of concern etched upon his features.

Do you:

- ❖ Approach him directly and explain the urgency of the matter? Turn to **24**.
- ❖ Wait patiently for him to finish his studies, respecting his focus? Turn to **23**.

23

You find a quiet corner nearby and sit, observing the Imam. He is utterly absorbed in the scroll, his lips moving silently as he reads. The minutes stretch on, perhaps a quarter of an hour passes. Finally, he sighs, his brow furrowed, and carefully rolls up the scroll. He then seems to sense your presence and turns towards you, his expression shifting from scholarly focus to gentle inquiry.

"Peace be upon you," he says softly. "I sensed a need for counsel. What troubles you, my child?"

Turn to **24**.

24

You greet the venerable Imam Tariq with respect and then, finding the words, you recount the strange and unsettling events you have witnessed and heard about in Asfaran. You mention the unnatural destruction, the unnerving whispers from below, the strange figure, and the blights. You describe the growing fear and the feeling that something ancient and malevolent is stirring beneath the surface of the city.

Imam Tariq listens with rapt attention, stroking his beard. As you speak of the whispers from below and the unnatural decay, his eyes widen slightly, and he gestures towards the scrolls around him.

"Your words confirm my gravest fears," he says, his voice low but firm. "For weeks, I have felt a darkness gathering, a spiritual dissonance that chills the soul. My studies of the oldest texts – writings passed down through generations, speaking of times before even the great Caliphates – speak of such omens. The unnatural destruction, the voices from the earth, the corruption of life itself... These are signs of a Shaytan, a powerful demon from the realms of shadow, attempting to break through into our world."

He leans forward, his gaze intense. "Such entities feed on discord, on fear, on the breaking of harmony. The conflicts of the outside world," he pauses, perhaps alluding to the Crusades or other strife, "only serve to weaken the veil between realms."

He gestures back to the scroll he was reading. "These texts speak of ancient wards, and of a banishment ritual performed by heroes of old. They hint at the location of a key to that ritual, perhaps an artifact or forgotten lore, hidden in ruins far from here... near a place known in antiquity as Kufa's Whisper, close to the contested frontiers."

Imam Tariq sighs, looking weary but resolute. "To face such a being, should it fully manifest, is beyond the strength of any one mortal. Even to retrieve the key requires courage and diverse skills. You are clearly one drawn to the light, brave enough to seek understanding. But you cannot face this darkness alone. Others, perhaps, are also stirring, sensing the growing threat. Be vigilant. Look for those who fight against this shadow, even if their path is different from your own. You will need allies if you are to confront this evil."

He has given you crucial information: the nature of the enemy, their potential goal, and the location of a possible solution. He has also given you a vital piece of advice: find allies. Your path now leads you back into the city, armed with this knowledge and the Imam's blessing, to continue your investigation and seek out those who might stand with you.

You thank Imam Tariq for his wisdom and counsel. You leave the peaceful confines of the Grand Masjid, returning to the still-uneasy streets of Asfaran.

Turn to **24a**.

24a

You are back in the bustling, yet subtly uneasy, streets of Asfaran. You carry the weight of the information you've gained.

You know you need allies, as the Imam advised, and the threat is real. The city is still tense, but no major incident is occurring *right now*. What do you do next?

Do you:

- ❖ Focus your investigation on areas where strange tremors or disturbances have been reported, seeking answers from the earth itself? Turn to **38**.
- ❖ Attempt to verify or gain more information about the rumors of a mysterious veiled operative or the city's underbelly contacts? Turn to **25**.

❖ Decide to patrol a key area of the city, perhaps a gate or a central plaza, where trouble is likely to erupt, hoping to encounter other individuals fighting the same darkness? Turn to **50**.

CHAPTER 3: SECRETS IN THE VEIL

A lone, cloaked, archer, perched silently on a rooftop overlooking the city's alleys at night. She is drawing her bow and looking intently into the shadows below.

25

The Grand Masjid offers spiritual solace, but perhaps the answers you seek are more... grounded. You leave the more respectable districts and venture into the city's underbelly – a maze of narrow streets, hidden courtyards, and establishments that operate away from the watchful eyes of the city guards. You venture into the less-lit alleys and bustling, unofficial markets where secrets are bought and sold as easily as silks and spices.

You discreetly ask around, mentioning the strange incidents and your desire to understand what is truly happening. Most people are wary, offering only shrugs or fearful glances. But eventually, your inquiries lead you to a specific, dimly lit corner near a spice warehouse after sundown. You meet a contact known to broker information. He is wrapped in a nondescript cloak, his eyes darting nervously.

"You seek understanding of the whispers and the blight?" he asks, his voice a low rasp. "Such knowledge is dangerous... and valuable. Some say a figure moves through the city like a phantom, seeing all, known only as 'The Shadow.' If you could find them... they might have answers." He gives you an appraising look. "But proving you're not a fool, or simply making it worth my while to point you even vaguely in their direction... that requires something."

Do you:

- ❖ Attempt to prove your capability with a display of skill or subtlety right now, hoping to impress the contact? Turn to **26**.
- ❖ Offer the contact a significant bribe to loosen their tongue? Turn to **27**.
- ❖ Decide this contact is untrustworthy or too risky, and look elsewhere for information about the 'Shadow'? Turn to **30**.

26

You decide that action speaks louder than coin. You need to show this contact you are competent and not easily dealt with. Thinking quickly, you identify a challenge – perhaps scaling a difficult wall nearby, vanishing into a dark alley silently, or disarming a visible (but harmless) trap on a merchant's nearby cart without being noticed.

You attempt your chosen feat. **Test your Skill**.

- ❖ If successful, turn to **32**.
- ❖ If unsuccessful, turn to **28**.

27

Coin speaks a universal language in this part of the city. You decide offering a bribe is the most direct way to get information from the contact. You subtly reach into your purse, preparing to offer a generous sum.

Will your attempt to bribe succeed? **Test your Luck**.

- ❖ If your Luck roll is less than or equal to your current LUCK score, turn to **32**.
- ❖ If your Luck roll is greater than your current LUCK score, turn to **29**.

28

Your attempt to prove your capability fails. Perhaps you slipped while climbing, made too much noise in the alley, or fumbled with the trap. The contact gives a snort of derision or a nervous glance. Your clumsiness or failure has either marked you as incompetent or drawn unwanted attention.

The contact quickly melts back into the shadows. You gain no information from him. Worse, your failure might have caused a minor injury (lose 1 Stamina) or alerted unseen watchers to your presence. You realise getting information here will be harder than you thought.

Turn to **31**.

29

Your attempt to bribe the contact goes badly. Perhaps you chose the wrong amount, or someone else was watching. The contact's eyes narrow, he snatches at your purse, and suddenly you feel a sharp bump as someone else rushes past you. Your purse is gone! You've been robbed by an unseen pickpocket, likely in league with the contact who has vanished.

The contact is gone, and you have nothing to show for it but a lighter coin pouch.

Turn to **31**.

30

You sense that the contact is untrustworthy or that his price is too high, whether in coin or risk. You politely decline and move on. Finding reliable information in the underbelly without a known contact is difficult and dangerous. You spend time navigating smoky taverns, asking questions in guarded whispers, and keeping a wary eye on the shadows.

This approach requires significant street smarts and discretion. Attempt to find a more reliable, albeit harder to access, source of information about 'The Shadow'. **Test your Skill.** This is a difficult task.

- ❖ If successful, turn to **33**.
- ❖ If unsuccessful, turn to **31**.

31

Your initial attempt to gain information in the underbelly has met with setback. You're no closer to finding answers. The city's lower levels are dangerous and unforgiving. Getting trustworthy information here requires perseverance and caution.

Despite the difficulty, you persist, spending more time and risking more encounters in the dangerous alleys. Eventually, through sheer persistence or a stroke of minor luck (reroll your starting Luck, if it's higher use that for now, otherwise no change), you find a different, less prominent contact. This one is even more nervous but gives you a cryptic lead – a specific time, a specific rooftop near the old spice district, a signal you must give. "If they are there," the contact whispers, "and if they deem you worthy... perhaps they will meet."

This path is risky. You could be meeting 'The Shadow,' or you could be walking into an ambush.

Turn to **34**.

32

Your display of skill or your generous bribe has impressed the contact. He gives a curt nod. "You are not a fool, then," he admits, or, "Gold speaks clearly."

He lowers his voice. "There are rumours... of a figure who sometimes appears on the rooftops near the old spice exchange, just after the evening call to prayer. They say she watches the city from above. Go there tonight. Look for a solitary figure near the highest point. Give a specific signal – a soft bird call, three times." He provides the specific call. "But be warned," he adds, his eyes serious. "Approach incorrectly, or be followed, and she will vanish... or worse. And if you see anyone else there... they are likely enemies looking for her."

He gives you the precise location and the signal. This is your chance to potentially meet 'The Shadow.' The risk is high, but the potential reward is great.

Turn to **34**.

33

Persistence pays off. After navigating the treacherous waters of the underbelly for a significant period, avoiding scams and suspicious figures, you manage to find a contact who seems slightly more reliable than the initial one, perhaps someone with a reputation for discretion rather than simple greed. This contact is harder to find but offers clearer, less cryptic instructions.

"There is a safehouse," they tell you quietly, providing a location in a less trafficked part of the city, disguised as an old, abandoned workshop. "Leave a specific token by the door," they instruct, describing it. "If it is taken, return here the next night at the same time. You may receive a message, or perhaps, if you are deemed trustworthy, you will be granted a meeting." This path feels slightly less impulsive than a rooftop rendezvous, suggesting a more established network.

You follow the instructions, leaving the token. Returning the next night, you find the token is gone, replaced by a small, rolled parchment. Inside is a simple, elegant message directing you to another discreet location – a small, quiet tea house known for its reclusive clientele, at a specific hour the following day. "Ask for the 'Silent Brew'," the message instructs. This seems to be the final step to a meeting.

Turn to **34**.

34

You follow the instructions you received to potentially meet 'The Shadow.' Whether you are heading to a specific rooftop after dark, watching an old workshop, or approaching a discreet tea house, the tension is palpable. You know that failure to be subtle, or being followed, could be disastrous.

Carefully, you navigate towards the location, trying to blend into the shadows, listen for unseen followers, and follow the instructions precisely.

This requires significant stealth and awareness. **Test your Skill**.

- If successful, turn to **35**.
- If unsuccessful, turn to **36**.

35

You have successfully made contact! You are now in the presence of 'The Shadow.'

The figure removes her outer cloak, revealing herself as a woman clad in practical, dark clothing, her face framed by a niqab that covers everything but her intense, intelligent eyes. She moves with unnerving grace, and you notice a bow case slung across her back, alongside quivers of various arrows, and the lean, muscular build of a martial artist. This is Zahra, the operative you heard whispers of.

She speaks calmly, her voice clear. "You seek answers regarding the disturbances in the city. You are not the first to sense the deeper wrongness." She confirms that the incidents are not random Jinn mischief, but are orchestrated, spreading fear and confusion. "There are those among the city's own who aid this darkness," she reveals, "opportunists or perhaps those deluded by promises of power. They are disrupting networks, sowing discord, weakening the city's defenses from within. And," she lowers her voice, "I have seen things... shapes moving in the dark that are not human, guiding the actions of these collaborators."

Her intelligence paints a picture of a coordinated attack, from mundane sabotage to something far more sinister. She is dedicated to protecting the city, using her unique skills to move unseen and strike from the shadows against these internal and external threats. She recognises your determination.

"This threat is growing," she concludes. "We cannot fight it alone. Others are also investigating, each with their own knowledge. A veteran soldier, perhaps, or a scholar of ancient lore, or even guardians from the old places of the earth. Their paths must converge if Asfaran is to be saved."

You have gained invaluable intelligence and found a powerful, if mysterious, ally in Zahra. You now understand the threat is not just supernatural, but also includes human agents. You leave the meeting place, knowing you are no longer alone in this fight.

Turn to **37**.

36

Your attempt to make contact fails disastrously! Perhaps you were followed, or you stumbled into a trap set by those searching for 'The Shadow,' or your signal was misunderstood.

Suddenly, figures emerge from the shadows! They are human, but move with a chilling efficiency, some armed with mundane weapons, others wielding simple daggers or bludgeons, but with a disturbing glint in their eyes – these must be the city collaborators! They have caught you!

COMBAT!
You are attacked by **TWO CITY COLLABORATORS**.

- ❖ **CITY COLLABORATOR 1**: SKILL 6, STAMINA 4
- ❖ **CITY COLLABORATOR 2**: SKILL 5, STAMINA 5

Fight them one at a time using the combat rules (see Introduction). Choose which one you attack first. Resolve combat round by round, rolling 2D6 for attack, comparing to SKILL, and dealing 2D6 damage on a hit. Remember to reduce your STAMINA if you are hit.

- ❖ If you defeat both City Collaborators: Turn to **37**.
- ❖ If your STAMINA reaches 0 during the fight: Turn to **37a**.

37

You are back in the bustling, yet subtly uneasy, streets of Asfaran. You carry the weight of the information you've gained – knowledge of a powerful Shaytan seeking to manifest, perhaps intelligence about human collaborators, or whispers of ancient wards being broken. You know you need allies, and the threat feels ever closer. The city is tense, but no major incident is occurring *right now*.

You know that seeking wisdom or hidden knowledge were paths to understanding. Now, perhaps, you must investigate the physical signs of this darkness, or place yourself where the conflict is most likely to erupt.

What do you do next?

- ❖ Focus your investigation on areas where strange tremors or disturbances have been reported, seeking answers from the earth itself? Turn to **38**.
- ❖ Decide to patrol a key area of the city, perhaps a gate or a central plaza, where trouble is likely to erupt, hoping to encounter other individuals fighting the same darkness? Turn to **50**.

37a

Your Stamina has reached 0, or your quest has ended in failure. You fought bravely, but the forces against you were too great. The darkness was too much, or a wrong choice led you to ruin. Your adventure ends here. The fate of Asfaran, and perhaps the world, is grim.

Perhaps another hero will take up the mantle and rise to face the darkness.

Start again from the beginning if you wish to try your luck (or skill) again.

Chapter 4: Dust and Duty

A rugged, powerful dwarf warrior standing firmly in a desolate, rocky mountain pass. He is gripping a large, formidable battle axe. His face is stern and weathered. We can see the harsh texture of the rocks and the emptiness of the landscape behind him.

38

You focus your investigation on areas where tremors have been felt or where reports mention unnatural changes to the stone or earth. This leads you towards the city's outskirts, closer to the rugged, ancient mountains that border the region. The ground feels strangely cold in places, and you notice cracks in the earth where there shouldn't be any.

As you follow a faint, almost imperceptible trail that leads into a less-visited gorge, you hear the sound of heavy impacts – like hammer on stone, but rhythmic and powerful. Rounding a bend, you see a stout figure hacking at a large boulder with a formidable battle axe. He is short, immensely muscular, with a thick beard woven with silver rings. This is no ordinary mountain dweller. This is a dwarf.

He notices you immediately, stopping his work and gripping his axe defensively. His gaze is wary and intense.

"State your purpose, stranger," he rumbles, his voice deep like stones rolling. "These lands are under my watch. And they are troubled. Are you part of the trouble, or do you feel it too?"

He is clearly suspicious. Do you:

- ❖ Approach carefully, explaining who you are and what you've learned about the darkness in Asfaran? Turn to **40**.
- ❖ Assume he might be hostile or connected to the earth's disturbances and prepare for a potential confrontation? Turn to **39**.

39

His wary stance makes you cautious. You hold your ground, ready for him to make a move. He lowers his axe slightly, his eyes narrowed. He seems to be assessing your readiness, not necessarily eager for a fight unless you provoke one.

He speaks again, his tone challenging. "You stand ready... but against what? Do you not understand the earth's pain? Prove you are not one of the things that gnaws at its roots!" He gestures with his axe towards the cracked ground.

You must convince him you are not an enemy. This will require a display of understanding or intent, or perhaps a feat that shows you are on the side of order, not chaos.

- ❖ Attempt to articulate your purpose clearly, focusing on the shared threat to the land and the city. **Test your Skill** (representing your ability to communicate effectively under pressure). If successful, turn to **40**. If unsuccessful, turn to **43**.
- ❖ Attempt a small, symbolic act against the source of the corruption near him (e.g., purifying a patch of corrupted earth if you have that ability, or striking a symbol of blight you see). **Test your Luck** (representing whether your act is correctly interpreted and effective). If successful, turn to **42**. If unsuccessful, turn to **44**.

40

You lower your guard slightly and explain your presence. You speak of the strange occurrences in Asfaran, the whispers from below, the spreading blight, and the information you've gained about a powerful dark force. You mention the unsettling feeling in the earth here and your search for answers about it.

The dwarf listens intently, his expression shifting from suspicion to grim understanding. "Hmph," he grunts when you finish. "Whispers from below... aye, we feel it in the deep places. The stone itself cries out. Ancient wards, buried long before your city was built, are being gnawed at. Things that should sleep forever are stirring."

He introduces himself as Jabbar, of the Stone-Guard, guardians of the deep places. "My kin feel the tremors, the unnatural heat, the foulness spreading through the very bones of the world," he says. "I came to see what was happening on the surface. The blight you speak of... it is connected. A sickness is seeping from below, guided by malice."

He sees the connection between the city's plight and the suffering of the earth. He looks at you with newfound respect. "You seek to fight this? Good. Too many surface-dwellers are blind. This 'Shaytan' your scholar speaks of... it taints the very foundation of this realm. I will stand against it. The Stone-Guard does not abandon its duty."

Jabbar, the axe-wielding dwarf, has joined your cause. He possesses ancient knowledge of the earth and things that dwell beneath it, and formidable strength.

Turn to **42**.

42

Your words or actions have convinced Jabbar. He sees that you are fighting the same darkness that threatens his people and the earth itself. He introduces himself as Jabbar of the Stone-Guard and confirms that the disturbances are linked to ancient wards being broken by a powerful, malevolent force from below. He agrees to join you, offering his strength, knowledge of the earth, and axe against the common enemy.

With Jabbar by your side, you feel more prepared to face the threats ahead. You have gained a powerful and knowledgeable ally.

Turn to **45**.

43

Your attempt to explain yourself to Jabbar fails. Perhaps your words were poorly chosen, or your nervousness made you seem deceitful. He growls, gripping his axe tighter. "Words are dust! I see no truth in yours. You trespass on suffering ground and speak riddles!" He looks ready to attack.

You must prove yourself through action!

- ❖ Attempt to quickly purify a small area of blight near you using whatever means you have (e.g. invoking faith, concentrating your will - requires a **Luck** roll). Success leads to **42**. Failure leads to **44**.
- ❖ Prepare for combat! **Test your Skill**. If successful, turn to **43a**. If unsuccessful, turn to **43b**.

43a

You successfully anticipate his first move and defend yourself, proving you are capable in a fight. Roll Initiative! While you don't want to defeat him, you must survive and show your strength. Fight Jabbar (Skill 8, Stamina 10). Survive 3 rounds of combat and he will pause, impressed by your tenacity. If you survive 3 rounds, turn to **40**. If your Stamina reaches 0, turn to **46**. If you somehow reduce his Stamina to 0, turn to **44**.

43b

You are caught off guard slightly as Jabbar lunges forward! He is fast for his size. He immediately hits you! Lose 4 Stamina. Roll Initiative and begin combat as in 43a. If you survive 3 rounds, turn to **40**. If your Stamina reaches 0, turn to **46**. If you reduce his Stamina to 0, turn to **44**.

44

Your attempts to reason with or impress Jabbar fail, or you were forced to subdue him. He sees you as an enemy or an incompetent fool who cannot understand the earth's plight. He either retreats into the mountains, leaving you alone and without his aid, or lies defeated. You have lost a potential ally and source of knowledge. The path of the Stone-Guard is closed to you for now.

You return towards Asfaran, the feeling of unease from the mountains now heavier. You must seek allies elsewhere.

Turn to **45**.

45

You have pursued the lead about the tremors and strange earth disturbances. You have either gained a powerful dwarven ally, Jabbar, or learned that this specific avenue of investigation has closed for you. As you head back towards Asfaran, or continue observing the situation from the city's edge, you sense that the situation is escalating rapidly. The distant sounds of the city seem more frantic, and the unnatural energy you felt earlier seems to be pulsing with increased intensity. The time for subtle investigation feels over.

It feels like the storm is finally breaking. You must return to the heart of Asfaran and place yourself where you can best confront the rising darkness, and perhaps find the other individuals who, like you, are fighting against it. All signs point to a critical point of conflict unfolding now within the city itself.

Turn to **50**.

46

Your Stamina has reached 0, or your quest has ended in failure. You fought bravely, but the forces against you were too great. The darkness was too much, or a wrong choice led you to ruin. Your adventure ends here. The fate of Asfaran, and perhaps the world, is grim.

Perhaps another hero will take up the mantle and rise to face the darkness.
Start again from the beginning if you wish to try your luck (or skill) again.

THE CRESCENT AND THE CRYPT

Chapter 5: The Gathering Storm

A moment of chaos in a city street, with partially visible stalls and fleeing figures. A monstrous, distorted supernatural creature is lashing out. We can see the heroes arriving – a shadow figure on a wall, a charging, axe-wielding shape.

50

Whether you decided to patrol a key area of Asfaran or returned to the city after investigating the tremors, you find yourself in a large, open area – perhaps a grand plaza near a city gate, or a wide street leading towards the city centre. The usual activity has stopped. The air is crackling with dark energy.

And then, chaos erupts.

From multiple points, figures charge into the open area. Some are clearly human – figures in rough, dark clothing, wielding crude weapons, eyes filled with unnatural malice (the collaborators Zahra spoke of, if you met her). Others are monstrous, their forms twisted and disturbing, appearing from shadows or emerging from cracks in the ground (minor demons or corrupted creatures). Leading them, or directing their movements, are larger, more powerful figures – perhaps a dark sorcerer, or a heavily armored knight whose form shimmers with unnatural energy.

Citizens scream and scatter. City guards are quickly overwhelmed. This is a coordinated assault, targeting a vital part of Asfaran.

You cannot stand idly by. You must fight!

Do you:

- ❖ Rush directly into the fray, engaging the nearest enemy to defend innocents or relieve pressure on the guards? Turn to **52**.
- ❖ Hold back for a moment, looking for a tactical advantage, a vulnerable enemy, or a way to assist without immediately engaging the main horde? Turn to **53**.

52

With a cry of defiance, you charge into the chaotic battle! You draw your weapon and engage the nearest enemy – a snarling, hunched creature with claws, or perhaps a human collaborator with unnaturally glowing eyes.

COMBAT!
You engage a **CORRUPTED CULTIST**.

- ❖ **CORRUPTED CULTIST:** SKILL 7, STAMINA 6

Fight the Corrupted Cultist using the combat rules.

- ❖ If you defeat the Corrupted Cultist: Turn to **55**.
- ❖ If your STAMINA reaches 0: Turn to **55c**.

53

Instead of immediately charging, you quickly scan the chaotic scene, seeking an opportunity. You look for weaknesses in the enemy ranks, a choke point you can defend, or perhaps a way to help pinned-down guards or civilians.

- ❖ Attempt to find a tactical advantage. **Test your Skill.**
    - ➢ If successful, turn to **54**.
    - ➢ If unsuccessful, turn to **52**. (You fail to find an opening and are forced to immediately engage the nearest threat).

54

You quickly identify a key point – perhaps a group of enemies attempting to break through a weak defensive line, or a clear shot at a minor leader figure, or a group of civilians trapped behind a collapsed structure. You can intervene here effectively!

- ❖ Do you rush to the aid of the city guards or civilians? Turn to **55a**.
- ❖ Do you attempt to strike at a key enemy target you've identified? Turn to **55b**.

55

You have defeated your immediate opponent or taken a decisive action! But the battle rages around you. You see other figures fighting against the tide of darkness – figures whose actions stand out from the panicked chaos.

You see a figure in a dark hood, their sword a blur, cutting down twisted creatures with practiced ease. Nearby, a stout, axe-wielding figure (Jabbar, if you met him) is cleaving through enemy ranks, roaring defiance. From a rooftop or elevated position, a swift, veiled figure (Zahra, if you met her) is firing precise arrows, dropping enemies with impossible accuracy. And near a struggling group of guards, a robed scholar (Imam Tariq, if you met him) is holding a glowing symbol, chanting powerful prayers that cause the dark forces to recoil.

These are the allies you have met, or perhaps heard of. And they are here, fighting the same fight. You are not alone!

A new wave of enemies pushes forward, targeting you and the other key figures resisting the assault.

COMBAT!
You are now part of a larger battle! You must fight alongside your potential allies against the incoming wave of enemies.

You will fight **THREE CORRUPTED CULTISTS**.

- **CORRUPTED CULTIST 1**: SKILL 7, STAMINA 6
- **CORRUPTED CULTIST 2**: SKILL 7, STAMINA 6
- **CORRUPTED CULTIST 3**: SKILL 7, STAMINA 6

Fight these enemies one at a time. Your allies are fighting their own battles nearby; they cannot directly assist you in this immediate combat section, but their presence holds back the main horde. Focus on defeating the enemies directly engaging you.

- If you defeat all three Corrupted Cultists: Turn to **56**.
- If your STAMINA reaches 0: Turn to **55c**.

55a

You rush towards the beleaguered guards or trapped civilians! Your timely intervention bolsters their defense. You fight alongside them against the enemies pinning them down.

Turn to **55**.

55b

You move to eliminate the target you identified – a minor leader or a creature holding a key position. Your decisive action briefly disrupts the enemy's attack pattern in this area.

COMBAT!
You engage a **DARK CAPTAIN**.

- **DARK CAPTAIN**: SKILL 8, STAMINA 8

Fight the Dark Captain using the combat rules.

- If you defeat the Dark Captain: Turn to **56**. (You rejoin the wider fight having eliminated a threat).
- If your STAMINA reaches 0: Turn to **55c**.

55c

Your Stamina has reached 0, or your quest has ended in failure. You fought bravely, but the forces against you were too great. The darkness was too much, or a wrong choice led you to ruin. Your adventure ends here. The fate of Asfaran, and perhaps the world, is grim.

Perhaps another hero will take up the mantle and rise to face the darkness.
Start again from the beginning if you wish to try your luck (or skill) again.

56

The wave of attackers targeting your immediate area is defeated! The tide of battle begins to turn as the defenders, bolstered by your efforts and those of the other powerful individuals, push back the remaining attackers. The human collaborators break and flee, while the monstrous entities dissolve into smoke or are destroyed. The immediate assault on this part of the city is repelled!

Weary, possibly wounded, you stand amidst the aftermath – scattered debris, fallen foes, and relieved but shaken citizens and guards. You look around and see the other key figures who were fighting the same battle.

If you haven't met them already, you now see them clearly:

- ❖ **Ali:** The veteran warrior, his sword stained, his expression grim but resolute. He stands amongst fallen foes, radiating competence.
- ❖ **Jabbar:** The stout dwarf, his axe dripping, standing firm like a mountain rock.
- ❖ **Zahra:** The veiled operative, descending from a rooftop or emerging from the shadows, her bow ready.
- ❖ **Imam Tariq:** The wise scholar, his face streaked with dust, but his eyes holding spiritual strength, tending to the wounded with blessings.

The immediate threat is gone, and your eyes meet those of the others who fought beside you. There is a shared understanding – you are all fighting the same darkness, and you cannot do it alone. Ali, as perhaps the most grounded and experienced in leading men, gestures for everyone to gather once the immediate danger has passed.

Turn to **58**.

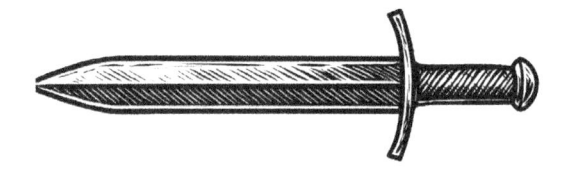

Chapter 6: Council of War

The four main heroes (hooded warrior, dwarf, Imam scholar, stealthy archer) gathered around a map on a table in a dimly lit, secure room.

58

In the aftermath of the assault, the city begins to recover, but the air remains tense. You and the other individuals who stood out in the fight are brought together in a secure location – perhaps a guarded chamber within the Masjid, or a noble's house dedicated to defence. You stand before Ali, the veteran warrior, who now seems to be taking charge.

He looks at each of you – the one who sought out wisdom (you, if you went to the Imam), the one who moved unseen through the shadows (you, if you went to the Underbelly), the one who came from the ancient mountains (Jabbar, now introduced if not met), and the one who has dedicated his life to the city's defense (Ali himself, introduced here). He also introduces the Imam, the scholar whose spiritual strength was vital, and Zahra, whose prowess in the shadows is clear.

"We have faced a shadow," Ali states grimly. "Not just men, but creatures of malice, guided by a dark power. My years fighting Crusader hordes prepared me for battle, but this... this was different. Unholy."

Imam Tariq steps forward, his voice calm despite the recent chaos. He speaks of the powerful Shaytan he found in the ancient texts, of its goal to manifest fully, feeding on the fear and conflict that plagues the land. He speaks of the ancient banishment ritual and the key to it, hidden near Kufa's Whisper.

Zahra confirms the Imam's fears from her perspective. "I have tracked the collaborators," she says, her voice low. "They serve something vast and ancient. They seek to break the city's will, to let the darkness in fully. They are just pawns, but dangerous pawns."

Jabbar, if present, adds his perspective. "The earth is sick," he rumbles. "The roots of the mountains cry out. Ancient wards are being undone from below. This 'Shaytan' gnaws at the very foundations of this world. The key the Imam speaks of... it might relate to those ancient bindings."

The situation is dire, but the path forward is clear. You have faced a common enemy, and now you have formed an unlikely alliance – warrior, dwarf, scholar, operative, and yourself. The key to stopping the full manifestation of the Shaytan lies in that ancient artifact or knowledge, wherever it is hidden near Kufa's Whisper. Retrieving it is the only hope.

"We must act swiftly," Ali says, looking at each of you. "While Asfaran tends its wounds, we must embark on this quest. It will be dangerous. The enemy knows we resist. Our path will likely take us through contested lands, corrupted areas, and whatever guardians protect that hidden place."

You all agree. This is your quest. The party is formed. Your adventure now truly begins.

Turn to **70**.

Part 2: The Serpent's Coil

Chapter 7: The Road to Kufa's Whisper

70

With the immediate crisis in Asfaran contained, your group departs the city. Your destination: the vicinity of Kufa's Whisper, a frontier town or perhaps the site of older settlements, said to lie near the ancient ruins holding the key to the banishment ritual. You travel together – yourself, Ali, Jabbar, Imam Tariq, and Zahra. Each brings unique skills, but the journey itself is fraught with peril. The lands between Asfaran and the frontier are often contested or wild.

You discuss the route. There are main roads, generally safer but longer and potentially patrolled by enemies (both human and supernatural), and less-traveled paths through hills or wilderness, shorter but riskier and less predictable.

Which route do you suggest the group take?

- ❖ Take the main road, relying on vigilance and strength in numbers. Turn to **72**.
- ❖ Attempt a shortcut through the less-travelled hills, relying on Zahra's tracking and stealth, and hoping to avoid major concentrations of enemies. Turn to **75**.

72

You choose the main road, hoping its relative safety will see you through. The road is wide but often winds through valleys or alongside rocky outcrops, providing potential ambush points. You travel for several days.

Mid-way through your journey along this road, you hear sounds ahead – the distinct ring of steel and shouts. It seems there's trouble.

- ❖ Do you proceed cautiously, preparing for a potential encounter? Turn to **74**.
- ❖ Do you try to ascertain the nature of the conflict ahead before revealing yourselves? Turn to **73**.

73

You signal the group to halt while you or Zahra (decide who is best suited – if you have high Skill, maybe you; otherwise, Zahra) attempts to scout ahead and see who is fighting.

- ❖ **Test your Skil**l (or Zahra's Skill, 8).
  - ➢ If successful, turn to **76**.
  - ➢ If unsuccessful, turn to **74**.

74

You fail to gather information and proceed towards the sounds of conflict. Rounding a bend in the road, you find yourselves facing a group of figures blocking the path! They are rough-looking bandits, perhaps mixed with a few human collaborators, preying on travelers. They see you, a well-armed group, as potential rich targets.
"Looks like coin and steel!" shouts their leader, grinning maliciously. "Get 'em!"

COMBAT!
You are attacked by **FOUR BANDITS**.

- ❖ **BANDIT 1**: SKILL 5, STAMINA 5

THE CRESCENT AND THE CRYPT

- ❖ **BANDIT 2**: SKILL 5, STAMINA 5
- ❖ **BANDIT 3**: SKILL 6, STAMINA 6
- ❖ **BANDIT 4**: SKILL 6, STAMINA 6

Fight the Bandits! Your allies (Ali, Jabbar, Zahra, Imam Tariq) fight alongside you, engaging enemies. You must defeat the four listed here directly engaging you. Resolve combat round by round.

- ❖ If you defeat all four Bandits: Turn to **76**.
- ❖ If your STAMINA reaches 0: Turn to **79a**.

75

You decide to take the less-traveled route through the hills. Zahra's tracking and navigation skills are invaluable here, guiding you through rough terrain and helping you avoid obvious dangers. However, the wilderness holds its own perils – not just wild animals, but pockets of corrupted energy or creatures drawn to the growing darkness.

As you traverse a narrow gorge, the air grows cold and heavy. Strange, thorny vines with unnatural crimson thorns grow from the rock. You feel a chilling presence.

- ❖ Attempt to navigate through the corrupted area cautiously, relying on Jabbar's knowledge of stone and earth to find a safe path. **Test your Luck**. If successful, turn to **77**. If unsuccessful, turn to **78**.
- ❖ Attempt to quickly pass through the area before whatever is here can fully manifest. **Test your Skill**. If successful, turn to **77**. If unsuccessful, turn to **79**.

76

If you fought, the bandits/patrol are defeated, leaving their bodies and perhaps some meager loot behind. If you scouted successfully, you might have witnessed a conflict that ended just before you arrived, or found a way around a dangerous group.

The main road has presented its challenges, but you have overcome them. You continue your journey towards Kufa's Whisper.

Turn to **80**.

77

Your caution and skill (or luck) see you through the corrupted gorge. Jabbar points out stable ground despite the blight, or you move swiftly enough to avoid attracting the worst of the lingering energies. You emerge from the area feeling shaken, but unharmed by the immediate supernatural threat. The path was difficult, but quicker.

Turn to **80**.

78

Your attempt to find a safe path through the corrupted area fails. The ground beneath you gives way slightly, or a pocket of dark energy flares up! You are momentarily engulfed in chilling negative energy. Lose 3 Stamina.

A low growl echoes from the rocks. A creature twisted by corruption has been drawn to you!

COMBAT!
You are attacked by a **CORRUPTED BEAST**.

- ❖ **CORRUPTED BEAST:** SKILL 7, STAMINA 7

Fight the Corrupted Beast using the combat rules. Your allies fight similar creatures nearby.

- ❖ If you defeat the Corrupted Beast: Turn to **80**.

- If your STAMINA reaches 0: Turn to **79a**.

79

Your attempt to move quickly through the corrupted area fails. You stumble, making noise, or accidentally brush against the foul thorns, which slash at you. Lose 2 Stamina. The noise and disturbance attract attention.
You are ambushed by creatures lurking in the blighted area!

COMBAT!
You are attacked by **TWO BLIGHTED STRANGLERS**.

- **BLIGHTED STRANGLER 1:** SKILL 6, STAMINA 5
- **BLIGHTED STRANGLER 2:** SKILL 6, STAMINA 5

Fight the Blighted Stranglers. Your allies engage similar enemies.

- If you defeat both Blighted Stranglers: Turn to **80**.
- If your STAMINA reaches 0: Turn to **79a**.

79a

Your Stamina has reached 0, or your quest has ended in failure. You fought bravely, but the forces against you were too great. The darkness was too much, or a wrong choice led you to ruin. Your adventure ends here. The fate of Asfaran, and perhaps the world, is grim.

Perhaps another hero will take up the mantle and rise to face the darkness.
Start again from the beginning if you wish to try your luck (or skill) again.

Chapter 8: Trails of Corruption

A section of landscape that is clearly corrupted by dark magic. Showing twisted, sickly plants, cracked and unnatural ground textures, strange symbols etched into the earth. The sky is dark and oppressive. There is a sense of blight, decay, and unease in the environment.

80

As you continue your journey, you notice the land growing increasingly unhealthy. The signs of corruption are more widespread now – twisted, leafless trees, discolored earth, unnatural silence from birds and insects. You are drawing closer to the source of the blight that touched Asfaran. The air feels heavy and oppressive.

You need to pass through this area to reach the vicinity of Kufa's Whisper and the ancient ruins. The path ahead is unclear and seems to be guarded by both natural hazards warped by the darkness and the creatures it has spawned.

Do you:

- ❖ Stick together as a group, proceeding with caution and relying on combined strength to overcome obstacles? Turn to **82**.
- ❖ Send Zahra or yourself ahead to scout the path and identify the safest route or immediate threats? Turn to **83**.

82

Your group moves forward together, weapons ready, eyes scanning the blighted landscape. The ground is treacherous, full of concealed roots and slippery patches of dark, foul-smelling moss. You face hazards along the way.

As you cross a small, dried-up creek bed, the ground beneath you suddenly gives way! It's a sinkhole, warped by unnatural energies!

- ❖ Attempt to leap back to solid ground. **Test your Skill**.
    - ➢ If successful, turn to **84**.
    - ➢ If unsuccessful, turn to **85**.

83

Zahra moves ahead, a silent shadow in the corrupted land, trying to discern the safest path through the blight. You use stealth and observation to map out the immediate area.

- **Test your Skill** (representing the success of the scouting attempt).
  - If successful, turn to **86**.
  - If unsuccessful, turn to **87**.

84

With a burst of agility, you leap back just as the sinkhole collapses. Dust and corrupted earth tumble into the darkness. You avoided the immediate danger, though your allies might need to find another way around the new pit. The path is still perilous.

Turn to **88**.

85

You are not quick enough! The ground gives way beneath you, and you tumble into the sinkhole! It's not deep enough to trap you completely, but you land hard on jagged rocks and corrupted roots. Lose 4 Stamina. Getting out is a struggle, and your allies have to help pull you up. That was a close call.

Turn to **88**.

86

Your scouting attempt is successful! You identify a path that seems less affected by the blight and avoids several obvious signs of lurking creatures or unstable ground. You guide the group safely along the route you've discerned. The going is still difficult, but you have bypassed the worst of the immediate hazards.

Turn to **89**.

87

Your scouting attempt fails. Perhaps you missed a crucial detail, or the corruption twisted the landscape in a way you didn't anticipate. You lead the group into a particularly heavily blighted area. The air here is thick with foulness, and you can feel the energy actively trying to drain your will and strength. Lose 2 Stamina immediately.

And something has noticed your intrusion. A group of creatures, their forms distorted and empowered by the surrounding darkness, emerges from the twisted vegetation!

COMBAT!
You are attacked by **THREE BLIGHTED SERVANTS**.

- ❖ **BLIGHTED SERVANT 1**: SKILL 7, STAMINA 6
- ❖ **BLIGHTED SERVANT 2**: SKILL 7, STAMINA 6
- ❖ **BLIGHTED SERVANT 3**: SKILL 7, STAMINA 7

Fight the Blighted Servants. Your allies assist, but you must defeat these three yourself.

- ❖ If you defeat all three Blighted Servants: Turn to **89**.
- ❖ If your STAMINA reaches 0: Turn to **89e**.

88

You have dealt with the immediate hazard of the sinkhole. As you continue carefully, you are confronted by another obstacle – a patch of land where the ground itself seems to writhe and shift, and dark, thorny vines lash out!

- ❖ Attempt to carefully navigate the shifting ground and lashing vines. **Test your Skill**. If successful, turn to **89a**. If unsuccessful, turn to **89b**.
- ❖ Attempt to burn away or purify the corrupted vines with a torch or holy symbol (if you possess one/are the Imam – requires a Luck roll to be effective). If successful, turn to **89c**. If unsuccessful, turn to **89d**.

89

Despite the perils of the corrupted land, you have made it through! Kufa's Whisper is now within reach, or perhaps you have reached its vicinity, a place of crumbled walls and overgrown foundations where the ancient ruins are said to lie. The feeling of oppression lessens slightly, but is replaced by a sense of anticipation and mystery. The key to stopping the Shaytan is hidden nearby, likely deep within those forgotten places.

Turn to **90**.

89a

You carefully pick your steps, anticipating the ground's shifts and ducking or deflecting the lashing vines. You make it across the hazardous patch without taking damage.

Turn to **89**.

89b

The ground lurches beneath you, and the thorny vines lash out with unnatural speed! You are struck by the corrupted vegetation. Lose 3 Stamina. You stumble but manage to push through the hazard.

Turn to **89**.

89c

You use a torch or holy symbol against the corrupted vines. By chance or providence, the heat or holy energy reacts violently with the dark magic animating them. The vines shrivel back, burning away into foul-smelling smoke. The shifting ground settles momentarily. You have cleared the path.

Turn to **89**.

89d

Your attempt to burn or purify the vines is ineffective. The dark magic is too strong here, or your method is incorrect. The vines continue to lash, and the ground remains unstable. You are forced to navigate it the hard way.

Turn to **89b**.

89e

Your Stamina has reached 0, or your quest has ended in failure. You fought bravely, but the forces against you were too great. The darkness was too much, or a wrong choice led you to ruin. Your adventure ends here. The fate of Asfaran, and perhaps the world, is grim.

Perhaps another hero will take up the mantle and rise to face the darkness.
Start again from the beginning if you wish to try your luck (or skill) again.

Chapter 9: The Crusader Front

A tense scene near a military encampment or patrol crossing. Heavily armoured Crusader soldiers standing guard, with distinctive helmets and shields.

90

You are now close to the ancient ruins near Kufa's Whisper. However, this region is also a frontier, contested territory where the influence of the Crusader kingdoms presses against the local lands. As you approach the area, you see signs of their presence – watchtowers in the distance, patrols on ridge lines, and perhaps the distant walls of a Crusader-held outpost or castle.

Your path to the ruins lies through, or dangerously close to, territory controlled or frequented by Crusader forces. While your primary enemy is the Shaytan, the ongoing conflict between your people and the Crusaders is a very real, very present danger. They see anyone from your side as a potential enemy.

Do you:

- ❖ Attempt to stealthily bypass the Crusader presence, sticking to the shadows and less-patrolled areas? Turn to **92**.
- ❖ Accept that a confrontation is likely and prepare to fight your way through any patrols or outposts you encounter? Turn to **93**.

92

You decide that avoiding conflict with the Crusaders is the wisest path, saving your strength for the darkness ahead. Relying on Zahra's expertise in stealth and reconnaissance, the group attempts to move through the area unseen, utilizing cover and darkness.

This is a tense and risky maneuver. You must avoid being spotted by watchful eyes. **Test your Skill** (representing the success of the group's combined stealth effort).

- ❖ If successful, turn to **95**.
- ❖ If unsuccessful, turn to **94**.

93

You decide that your group's strength is sufficient to handle any Crusader patrols you might encounter. You proceed with caution, but ready for battle, making your way towards the ancient ruins. It is not long before you spot a Crusader patrol ahead, blocking the most direct route to the ruins. They see you. Swords are drawn. "Halt, heathens!" cries their leader.

COMBAT!
You are attacked by **THREE CRUSADER SOLDIERS** and their **SERGEANT**.

- **CRUSADER SOLDIER 1**: SKILL 7, STAMINA 7
- **CRUSADER SOLDIER 2**: SKILL 7, STAMINA 7
- **CRUSADER SOLDIER 3**: SKILL 7, STAMINA 7
- **CRUSADER SERGEANT**: SKILL 8, STAMINA 8

Fight the Crusader Soldiers. Your allies fight alongside you. You must defeat these three directly.

- If you defeat all three Crusader Soldiers and their Sergeant: Turn to **96**.
- If your STAMINA reaches 0: Turn to **98**.

94

Your attempt at stealth fails! Perhaps you made a noise, were spotted by a lookout you missed, or tripped over a hidden obstacle. A shout rings out from a nearby watchtower or patrol! "Intruders!"
The Crusaders are alerted to your presence! Patrols converge on your location! You are forced into a fight you tried to avoid.

Turn to **93**

95

Your stealthy approach is successful! Moving under cover, using the terrain to your advantage, and following Zahra's guidance, you manage to slip past the main concentrations of Crusader forces. You see patrols in the distance, hear their shouted commands, but they do not see you. You have avoided conflict and are closer to the ruins.

Turn to **97**.

96

You have defeated the Crusader patrol! Their bodies lie on the ground. You quickly search them, taking any useful gear (add 1 point to your Luck). The sounds of the fight might attract more attention, so you know you must move quickly. Turn to **97**.

97

Whether you bypassed them or fought through them, you have dealt with the immediate threat of the Crusader presence. The path to the ancient ruins is now clearer. In the distance, perhaps nestled in a hidden valley or on a plateau, you see the crumbling stones of what was once a significant structure – a fortress, a temple, or maybe a tomb. It feels ancient, silent, and perhaps... waiting. This must be the location of the key you seek.

Turn to **100**.

98

Your Stamina has reached 0, or your quest has ended in failure. You fought bravely, but the forces against you were too great. The darkness was too much, or a wrong choice led you to ruin. Your adventure ends here. The fate of Asfaran, and perhaps the world, is grim.

Perhaps another hero will take up the mantle and rise to face the darkness.
Start again from the beginning if you wish to try your luck (or skill) again.

CHAPTER 10: DUNGEON OF THE DJINN-KINGS

A dark, mysterious passage within ancient ruins. Crumbling stone walls with old carvings and strange symbols. A trap has been triggered – with darts shooting from the wall,

100

You have reached the ancient ruins near Kufa's Whisper. The structure is imposing even in its decay, built of massive, weathered stones etched with symbols you don't entirely recognise, though Imam Tariq or Jabbar might identify them as belonging to a long-vanished era or a forgotten people. The entrance is difficult to access – blocked by rubble, sealed by a heavy stone door, or simply well-hidden. The air around the ruins feels heavy, carrying a faint hum of lingering power, not entirely dark, but certainly potent and old.

You need to find a way inside.

Do you:

- ❖ Attempt to force open the most obvious (but blocked) entrance, relying on strength? Turn to **102**.
- ❖ Search for a hidden or less obvious entrance, relying on observation and cunning? Turn to **103**.

102

You decide the direct approach is best. You and perhaps Jabbar (if he is with you) attempt to move the heavy rubble or force open the massive stone door blocking the main entrance. This requires brute strength and coordinated effort.

- ❖ **Test your Skill** (representing your physical strength and the success of the effort). If successful, turn to **104**. If unsuccessful, turn to **101a**.

103

You decide that brute force is unlikely to work, or too noisy. You begin to search around the perimeter of the ruins, looking for a concealed doorway, a weak point in the wall, or a passage hidden by overgrown vegetation. Zahra is particularly adept at this type of search and assists you.

Test your Skill (representing your observation and search ability). If successful, turn to **104**. If unsuccessful, turn to **103a**.

104

Success! Whether you shifted the rubble enough to create a passage, found a hidden mechanism to move the stone door, or located a concealed entrance along the wall, you have found a way inside the ancient ruins.

The air within is cool and stale, smelling of dust and forgotten ages. Corridors stretch into darkness, and strange, faded murals or carvings cover the walls. You step inside, your allies following.

The entrance seals behind you. You are in the Dungeon of the Djinn-Kings.

Turn to **105**.

101a

Your attempt to force the main entrance fails. The rubble is too heavy, or the door is magically sealed or simply too well-jammed. Your efforts make a lot of noise but yield no results. You also strain yourself in the attempt. Lose 1 Stamina.

You must now try another approach. You should search for a hidden entrance instead.

Turn to **103**.

103a

Your search for a hidden entrance is unsuccessful. The walls seem solid, the vegetation conceals nothing but stone. You can't find any secret passages or weak points. Your allies look towards you expectantly.

Perhaps the main entrance wasn't as impossible as it seemed, or maybe you missed something obvious. You need to try a different approach or look again.

- ❖ Attempt to force open the main entrance (Turn to **102**).
- ❖ Try searching for a hidden entrance again (requires a Luck roll to see if you spot something you missed. If successful, turn to **104**. If unsuccessful, turn to **103b**).

103b

You search again, but still find nothing. The ruins seem determined to keep you out. You are starting to feel frustrated and perhaps a little unnerved by the silent resistance of the structure. Time is potentially running short.

Your allies suggest a different approach. Imam Tariq might suggest looking for spiritual or magical wards, or Jabbar might point out geological features that could conceal a passage.

- ❖ Trust the Imam's insight (requires a Luck roll, guided by faith). If successful, turn to 104. If unsuccessful, turn to 101a (The spiritual ward suggests the main door is the way, though still sealed).
- ❖ Trust Jabbar's insight (requires a Skill roll, guided by earthly knowledge). If successful, turn to **104**. If unsuccessful, turn to **101a**.

105

You are now inside the Dungeon of the Djinn-Kings. The air is heavy, and a faint, unnatural echo follows your movements. The path ahead is dark and leads deeper into the structure. You proceed cautiously.

Suddenly, a click sounds underfoot! It's a trap! Spikes begin to shoot from the walls!

- ❖ Attempt to quickly avoid or disarm the trap. **Test your Skill**. If successful, turn to **106**. If unsuccessful, turn to **107**.

106

With a burst of agility or a flash of insight, you react just in time! You leap over the collapsing floor, duck under the spikes. The trap is sprung, but you have avoided its effects! Your allies also manage to avoid it thanks to your warning.

Turn to **108**.

107

You are not quick enough! The trap hits you! Spikes pierce your armour. Lose 4 Stamina. You are hurt, but manage to recover before the trap can finish you. Your allies avoid the worst of it, but are shaken. Turn to **108**.

108

You have survived the trap, though possibly wounded. The path ahead leads through more dark corridors and chambers. You encounter signs that this place is not empty – strange claw marks on walls, unsettling whispers that seem to come from the stone, or perhaps the remains of previous intruders, twisted into grotesque forms.

You enter a large chamber filled with broken pillars and a sense of oppressive stillness. In the centre, guarding the passage beyond, is a creature warped by the lingering energies of this place – a Restless Guardian!

COMBAT!
You are attacked by a **RESTLESS GUARDIAN.**

- ❖ **RESTLESS GUARDIAN**: SKILL 8, STAMINA 12

Fight the Restless Guardian! Your allies fight alongside you, but you must defeat this entity yourself.

- ❖ If you defeat the Restless Guardian: Turn to **110**.
- ❖ If your STAMINA reaches 0: Turn to **109**.

109

Your Stamina has reached 0, or your quest has ended in failure. You fought bravely, but the forces against you were too great. The darkness was too much, or a wrong choice led you to ruin. Your adventure ends here. The fate of Asfaran, and perhaps the world, is grim.

Perhaps another hero will take up the mantle and rise to face the darkness.
Start again from the beginning if you wish to try your luck (or skill) again.

110

The Restless Guardian crumbles into dust and dissipates into shadow. The path forward is now open. You proceed deeper into the ruins. The architecture becomes stranger, hinting at beings not entirely human or even mundane who once dwelt here.

You reach a corridor whose walls are covered in murals depicting figures performing rituals or battling monstrous shapes. At the end of the corridor, a heavy, stone door is sealed, but not by force — it seems to require a sequence or a key, hinted at by the murals. One section of the mural seems particularly relevant, showing symbols in a specific order.

To open the door, you must interpret the mural and activate the symbols in the correct sequence. **Test your Skill** (representing your ability to decipher the ancient symbols and process the visual information, perhaps aided by Imam Tariq's knowledge of ancient lore or Jabbar's understanding of ancient construction/wards).

- ❖ If successful, turn to **112**.
- ❖ If unsuccessful, turn to **111**.

111

You study the mural, trying to understand the sequence of symbols, but their meaning is obscure, the depictions confusing. You try pressing a few symbols on the door, but nothing happens, or a minor ward zaps you (lose 1 Stamina). You cannot figure it out.

- ❖ Try to interpret the mural again. **Test your Luck**. If successful, turn to **112**. If unsuccessful, turn to **111a**.
- ❖ Perhaps there is another way past the door? Search for an alternative route (**Test your Skill**). If successful, turn to **113**. If unsuccessful, turn to **111b**.

111a

Despite focusing, you still cannot decipher the sequence from the mural. The symbols remain stubbornly cryptic. You are stuck at this door unless you can find another way around it.

Turn to **111b**.

111b

Your search for an alternative route is unsuccessful. The corridor seems solid, no secret passages or weak points are apparent. The only way forward seems to be through this sealed door. You are trapped unless you can figure out the puzzle.

Your allies offer suggestions. Imam Tariq tries to remember similar symbols from his texts. Jabbar examines the stonework for mechanical secrets. Ali suggests brute force (though it seems unlikely). Zahra looks for ways to climb over or bypass the door itself (also unlikely).

You must focus on the mural and the door again. **Test your Skill** one last time. This is a critical moment.

- ❖ If successful, turn to **112**.
- ❖ If unsuccessful, turn to **111c**.

111c

Despite your efforts and the help of your allies, you cannot decipher the mural or find a way past the sealed door. The secrets of the Djinn-Kings remain locked away, and your quest is halted here. You are trapped in the ruins, unable to proceed to the information you need. Without the key to the banishment ritual, Asfaran is doomed.

Turn to **116**.

112

Success! You have deciphered the sequence from the mural! You step up to the stone door and carefully press the symbols in the correct order. With a deep grinding sound, the heavy door slowly slides open, revealing the passage beyond.
You have overcome the guardian and the puzzle. The path ahead is clear, leading into the deepest part of the ruins.

Turn to **114**.

113

Your search for an alternative route is successful! Perhaps you found a narrow fissure in the wall, a passage concealed by a waterfall of dust, or a climbable section leading over the door. It was difficult, but you found a way around the puzzle.

Turn to **114**.

114

You pass through the now-open door or the alternative route. You are in a large, central chamber, perhaps the heart of the ruins. It is filled with relics of a forgotten age. In the center, atop a raised dais, are several large, stone tablets or an ancient sarcophagus, covered in writing and strange carvings. This must be where the key to the ritual is hidden, or where the crucial knowledge resides.

However, the chamber is not empty. Standing guard, or perhaps bound to protect the knowledge within, are powerful entities –

ancient, powerful remnants of the Djinn-Kings' era, enslaved Djinns!

COMBAT!
You are attacked by **TWO ANCIENT DJINNS**.

- **ANCIENT DJINN 1**: SKILL 9, STAMINA 10
- **ANCIENT DJINN 2**: SKILL 9, STAMINA 10

Fight the Ancient Djinns. These are tough opponents. Your allies fight similar threats or hold back other dangers in the chamber, allowing you to focus on these two.

- If you defeat both Ancient Djinns: Turn to **115**.
- If your STAMINA reaches 0: Turn to **116**.

115

The Ancient Djinns are defeated, their forms dissipating and crumbling to dust. The chamber is silent once more, save for your heavy breathing. The path to the central dais is open.

You approach the stone tablets or sarcophagus. They are covered in writing in the same ancient script as the murals outside. This is it – the forgotten knowledge, the key to the banishment ritual against the Shaytan.

Turn to **130**.

116

Your Stamina has reached 0, or your quest has ended in failure. You fought bravely, but the forces against you were too great. The darkness was too much, or a wrong choice led you to ruin. Your adventure ends here. The fate of Asfaran, and perhaps the world, is grim.

Perhaps another hero will take up the mantle and rise to face the darkness.

Start again from the beginning if you wish to try your luck (or skill) again.

Chapter 11: The Scholar's Revelation

130

You stand before the ancient tablets or the sarcophagus containing the knowledge you sought. The writing is complex, in a language used millennia ago. It pulses faintly with dormant energy. This is the culmination of your journey so far – the potential means to fight the looming darkness.

You need to decipher the text. This requires significant scholarly skill and patience.

Do you:

- ❖ Attempt to decipher the text yourself, relying on any knowledge of ancient languages you possess? **Test your Skill**. If successful, turn to **135**. If unsuccessful, turn to **131**.
- ❖ Ask Imam Tariq to decipher the text? Turn to **135**.

131

You try to read the ancient script, but it is too difficult. The symbols are confusing, their meaning elusive. You can make out only fragmented words or phrases, nothing coherent enough to be useful. You feel frustrated by your inability to grasp the knowledge before you.

Turn to **132**.

132

You cannot decipher the text alone. You look at your allies. Imam Tariq is clearly the most qualified for this task.

Do you ask Imam Tariq to attempt to decipher the text?

- ❖ Yes, ask him. Turn to **135**.
- ❖ No, decide to look for visual clues in the carvings instead, hoping they explain the ritual (requires a Skill test). If successful, turn to **136**. If unsuccessful, turn to **133**.

133

You try to glean information from the carvings surrounding the text, looking for depictions of the ritual, but they are too abstract or damaged by time. They provide no clear instructions or understanding. You are no closer to the key.

Turn to **134**.

134

You are at an impasse. You cannot read the text, and the carvings are unclear. The knowledge is right here, but you cannot access it.
Your allies urge you to let the Imam try. His expertise is needed.

Turn to **135**.

135

Imam Tariq steps forward. His eyes light up with recognition, though also trepidation, as he examines the ancient script.
"These are indeed the writings of the Pious Predecessors," he murmurs, "those who bound this powerful Shaytan in ages past."

He spends a significant amount of time poring over the text, his lips moving silently, occasionally gasping or nodding. The air in the chamber seems to grow colder, as he reads — the energy of the ancient knowledge reacting to his presence.

Finally, he looks up, his face pale but resolute. "I have found it," he says. "The full banishment ritual. It requires a specific confluence of spiritual supplications and Divine intervention. And it must be performed at a place of immense faith and power, where the veil between realms is already thin... and strong enough to contain the banishment."

He pauses, his eyes fixed on yours. "The texts are clear. The ritual must be performed in The Grand Masjid of Asfaran itself. At the heart of its prayer hall, during the hour of the Fajr (dawn) prayer, before the full light of the morning."

He looks grave. "But there is more. The texts also warn that if the Shaytan knows the ritual is being attempted, it will focus all its power, and its earthly agents, on that location, at that time, to prevent it. The Shaytan's influence has been spreading, and it knows we are seeking this knowledge. It will anticipate our move."

He looks towards Asfaran, far in the distance. "Asfaran... and specifically the Grand Masjid... will be under assault. The Shaytan will likely orchestrate a full-scale attack to prevent the ritual. We must return. And we must fight our way to the heart of the Masjid, and protect the ritual as I perform it."

You have the knowledge, but the task ahead is terrifyingly clear. You must race back to Asfaran, fight your way into the besieged Masjid, and defend Imam Tariq as he performs the only ritual that can banish the Shaytan. The final battle will be at the heart of your home.

Turn to **140**.

136

Your attempt to understand the carvings yields some results! While you can't read the text, the depictions show figures gathering, symbols glowing, and a large, shadowy form being pushed back. You discern that the ritual involves gathering at a significant location at a specific time, using spiritual supplications. The imagery strongly suggests a place of worship or spiritual significance. You also see depictions that look unsettlingly like the minarets and domes of Asfaran.

You piece together the clues from the carvings and the Imam's initial knowledge about the Shaytan. The ritual must be performed back in Asfaran, likely at the Grand Masjid. However, without reading the full text, you might be missing crucial details, such as the exact time, the required celestial alignment, or the warning about the Shaytan's counter-attack. **Test your Luck.**

- ❖ If successful, turn to **135a**.
- ❖ If unsuccessful, turn to **137**.

135a

In a flash of insight, the meaning becomes clear! You point out details in the carvings – a specific pattern that aligns with the rising sun at a particular angle. Combined with the images of the Masjid-like structure, you suddenly understand the exact time (dawn, Fajr prayer) and location (Grand Masjid, Asfaran) for the ritual. You also notice unsettling depictions of chaos and destruction surrounding the ritual site in the carvings, suggesting the ritual will be contested. You have intuited the core message, including the warning!

Turn to **135**

137

You have pieced together that the ritual must be performed in Asfaran, likely at the Grand Masjid. This is crucial information! However, you were unable to grasp the finer details from the carvings – the exact timing, or, most critically, the warning that the Shaytan will attack the ritual site directly. You believe returning to Asfaran and going to the Masjid is the objective. You tell your allies your findings. Imam Tariq is concerned you might be missing details but agrees Asfaran is the most likely location. You decide you must return immediately.

Turn to **138**.

138

You gather your group and quickly leave the ancient ruins, beginning the long journey back to Asfaran. The journey back through the corrupted lands and contested frontiers will be just as dangerous, perhaps more so now that you carry the key knowledge. You press on with urgency, knowing that time is critical.

Turn to **140**.

PART 3: THE CRESCENT ASCENDANT
CHAPTER 12: SIEGE OF THE HOLY PLACE

140

The journey back to Asfaran is a blur of urgency, danger, and exhaustion. You navigate the perilous lands once more, facing lingering threats, but driven by the knowledge you carry. As you finally crest the last hill overlooking the city, a gasp escapes your lips, and likely those of your allies.

Asfaran is under siege.

Not by a conventional army. The familiar banners of Crusader forces are there, yes, but their ranks are swollen and interspersed with dark, unnatural shapes – twisted creatures, hulking brutes, and figures radiating malevolence. Dark energy crackles in the air around the city walls. And all the attacking forces seem to be focused on one area: the Grand Masjid. Smoke rises from surrounding buildings, and the sounds of battle echo across the plains.

The Shaytan anticipated your discovery. It is attempting to utterly overwhelm the heart of faith in the city, to prevent the banishment ritual at the very location and time it is meant to take place. The Fajr (dawn) prayer is not far off. You have arrived just in time... or perhaps, terrifyingly late.

Turn to **141**.

141

The scale of the attack is immense. The city walls are being assaulted, but the main force is clearly directed at breaking through to the Masjid. You see valiant defenders – city guards, civilians who have taken up arms – fighting back, but they are hard-pressed by the sheer number and unnatural power of the attackers.
Getting to the Grand Masjid through the chaos and the enemy lines will be incredibly difficult. You need to breach the attacking forces and reach the heart of the siege. Your goal is to get Imam Tariq, and yourselves, to the main prayer hall inside the Masjid to perform the ritual as dawn approaches.

Do you:
- ❖ Attempt a risky infiltration, using stealth and agility to slip through the enemy lines and the city's back ways, aiming directly for the Masjid? Turn to **142**.
- ❖ Attempt to cut a direct, brutal path through the attacking forces, relying on your group's combat prowess to smash through the siege lines and reach the Masjid? Turn to **143**.

Chapter 13: Infiltration and Assault

142

Recognising the sheer numbers of the enemy, you opt for stealth. Under the guidance of Zahra, the group attempts to use the confusion of the siege as cover, moving through less-guarded alleys, across rooftops, and potentially utilising hidden passages. Your goal is to reach the Masjid perimeter unseen.

This is a complex and dangerous maneuver. You must avoid patrols, lookouts, and unexpected pockets of resistance. **Test your Skill** (representing the success of the group's combined stealth and navigation). This is a difficult task due to the widespread chaos.

- ❖ If successful, turn to **145**.
- ❖ If unsuccessful, turn to **144**.

143

You decide the fastest, most direct path to the Masjid is straight through the enemy lines, relying on your group's formidable combat abilities. With Ali leading the charge and Jabbar at the forefront, you smash into the attacking forces surrounding the Masjid district. It's a brutal, desperate fight.

You immediately engage a group of attackers blocking your path!

COMBAT!
You are attacked by **TWO CRUSADER BRUTES** and **TWO CORRUPTED HORRORS**.

- ❖ **CRUSADER BRUTE 1**: SKILL 8, STAMINA 9
- ❖ **CRUSADER BRUTE 2**: SKILL 8, STAMINA 9
- ❖ **CORRUPTED DJINN 1**: SKILL 9, STAMINA 8
- ❖ **CORRUPTED DJINN 2**: SKILL 9, STAMINA 8

Fight these four enemies! Your allies fight similar threats nearby, clearing a path, but you must defeat these directly.

- ❖ If you defeat all four enemies: Turn to **146**.
- ❖ If your STAMINA reaches 0: Turn to **149**.

144

Your infiltration attempt fails! You are spotted by an enemy lookout, or stumble into a patrol in an alley, or a collapsing building blocks your path and forces you into the open. The enemy knows where you are!

They converge on your position, forcing you into a direct confrontation you tried to avoid. You are now fighting your way through the siege lines.

Turn to **143**

145

Your infiltration is successful! Moving like ghosts through the chaos, you manage to slip past the main enemy concentrations. You see and hear the battle, but you avoid direct engagement. You have reached the outer perimeter of the Grand Masjid itself, which is still under heavy assault but not yet fully breached. The main door is likely sealed, or heavily defended from inside.

You need to get *inside* the Masjid.

Do you:

- ❖ Look for a less obvious entry point into the Masjid itself – perhaps a side door, a window, or even a drainpipe or minaret access point (requires a Skill test)? If successful, turn to **147**. If unsuccessful, turn to **145a**.
- ❖ Attempt to join the defenders at a fortified entrance and fight your way inside with them (requires engaging any enemies immediately outside)? Turn to **145b**.

145a

Your search for a hidden entry point into the Masjid fails. The building is solid, secured against intrusion, or the areas you can reach are heavily guarded. You can't find a discreet way in quickly.

Turn to **145b**.

145b

You are forced to approach one of the more obvious entry points into the Masjid, likely defended by a mix of last-stand city guards and the first wave of attackers trying to breach it. You must fight your way through the enemies immediately outside this entry point to gain access.

COMBAT!
You are attacked by **TWO CULT LEADERS** and **ONE SHADOW SPAWN**.

- ❖ **CULT LEADER 1**: SKILL 8, STAMINA 7
- ❖ **CULT LEADER 2**: SKILL 8, STAMINA 7
- ❖ **SHADOW SPAWN**: SKILL 9, STAMINA 9

Fight these enemies. Your allies are with you, fighting to get through, but you focus on these.

- ❖ If you defeat all three enemies: Turn to **147**.
- ❖ If your STAMINA reaches 0: Turn to **149**.

146

You have fought a brutal battle, cutting a swathe through the attacking forces! Your path is littered with fallen enemies. You have smashed your way to the perimeter of the Grand Masjid! Like the stealth path, the Masjid itself is still standing but under heavy assault.

Turn to **147**.

147

You have made it to the Grand Masjid and found a way inside, whether through a hidden entry or by fighting through a breached point! You are now within the outer sections of the holy building. The sounds of battle are muffled but still present. Inside, you encounter desperate defenders, perhaps finding yourselves in a side chamber or corridor.

You need to reach the main prayer hall, the heart of the Masjid, where Imam Tariq must perform the ritual. The path is not easy; the enemy has breached the outer parts of the building, and defenders are fighting delaying actions. You encounter resistance within the Masjid itself.

COMBAT!
You are attacked by **THREE SHADOW INFESTED** (creatures that have infested the building).

- ❖ **SHADOW INFESTED 1**: SKILL 7, STAMINA 6
- ❖ **SHADOW INFESTED 2**: SKILL 7, STAMINA 7
- ❖ **SHADOW INFESTED 3**: SKILL 8, STAMINA 6

Fight these enemies within the confines of the Masjid. Your allies fight alongside you, clearing the path to the prayer hall.

- ❖ If you defeat all three enemies: Turn to **148**.
- ❖ If your STAMINA reaches 0: Turn to **149**.

148

You clear the immediate path! You press on, navigating through contested corridors and chambers within the Masjid, following the most direct route to the main prayer hall. You pass scenes of desperate defense and sacred space being desecrated.

Finally, you burst into the vast, central prayer hall. It is not empty. The Shaytan's influence is strongest here, twisting the holy space. And at the far end, near the Mihrab (prayer niche indicating direction of Makkah), stands the orchestrator of this final assault – an agent of the Shaytan, its Herald, preventing anyone from reaching the ritual site.

Turn to **150**.

149

Your Stamina has reached 0, or your quest has ended in failure. You fought bravely, but the forces against you were too great. The darkness was too much, or a wrong choice led you to ruin. Your adventure ends here. The fate of Asfaran, and perhaps the world, is grim.

Perhaps another hero will take up the mantle and rise to face the darkness.
Start again from the beginning if you wish to try your luck (or skill) again.

CHAPTER 14: THE HEART OF THE STORM

The final climactic battle inside the core of the Masjid. The powerful Shaytan's Herald looms over the heroes.

150

You stand in the heart of the Grand Masjid, the main prayer hall. It should be a place of peace and prayer, but it is filled with crackling dark energy. The air is thick with malevolence, and the beautiful architecture is marred by shadows and unsettling whispers. Near the mihrab, where Imam Tariq must perform the banishment ritual, stands a powerful enemy – the Shaytan's Herald, a terrifying figure radiating dark power.

Imam Tariq wastes no time. He moves towards the designated spot, producing the ancient texts you found in the ruins. He begins chanting Words of Power of the banishment ritual.

The Shaytan's Herald roars, its attention focused on the Imam. It will do everything in its power to disrupt the ritual and destroy you all!

This is the final confrontation! The ritual requires time and concentration. Imam Tariq must be protected for **3 full rounds** of intense battle as he completes the banishment!

BOSS FIGHT!
You face the **SHAYTAN'S HERALD**.

- **SHAYTAN'S HERALD:** SKILL 10, STAMINA 25

This enemy is powerful! Roll for combat each round against its SKILL 10. If you hit, roll 2D6 damage. If it hits you, roll 2D6 damage and subtract from your STAMINA.

The Ritual:

- At the end of each round, after you and the Herald have attacked, Imam Tariq makes progress on the ritual.
- However, the Herald will attempt to disrupt him. At the start of each round (before attacks), **Test your Luck**. If successful, turn to **151**. If unsuccessful, turn to **152**.

Round 1: Begin combat against the Shaytan's Herald. Resolve attacks. **Test your Luck** for ritual disruption. Turn to **153**.

Round 2: Continue combat. Resolve attacks. **Test your Luck** for ritual disruption. Turn to **154**.

Round 3: Continue combat. Resolve attacks. **Test your Luck** for ritual disruption. Turn to **155**.

151

Imam Tariq is able to continue the ritual despite the chaos! Your efforts or perhaps divine protection shielded him from the Herald's disruptive power this round. The ritual progresses.

Proceed with combat for the current round. After attacks, move to the section number for the end of that round (**153**, **154**, or **155**).

152

The Shaytan's Herald focuses its malevolent energy on Imam Tariq! The ritual is disrupted! The Imam falters, the chanting breaks!

The Shaytan's Herald gains power from this disruption! Increase its SKILL by 1 for the rest of the fight (maximum 12). The Herald also immediately makes an extra attack against you this round! Resolve that attack (roll 2D6, compare to your SKILL, deal 2D6 damage on a hit).

After the extra attack, proceed with normal combat for the current round. After attacks, move to the section number for the end of that round (**153**, **154**, or **155**).

153

Round 1 is complete. The Shaytan's Herald is wounded (hopefully), and Imam Tariq has progressed the ritual (hopefully not disrupted). The Herald is still standing, radiating power. Dawn is drawing nearer outside.

Proceed to Round 2. Turn back to **150** for the start of Round 2.

154

Round 2 is complete. The battle is fierce, you are likely wounded, and the Herald is weakened, but still deadly. Imam Tariq's chanting is growing louder, more urgent. The air in the hall vibrates with opposing energies.

Proceed to Round 3. Turn back to **150** for the start of Round 3.

155

Round 3 is complete! You have survived the Herald's attacks and dealt damage. Imam Tariq's chanting reaches a crescendo!

Now, you must make one final, desperate strike, or hold the Herald at bay for just a moment longer while the ritual is completed!

- ❖ Attempt a final, powerful attack on the Shaytan's Herald. **Test your Skill.** If successful, turn to **156**. If unsuccessful, turn to **157**.
- ❖ Attempt to use your Luck to ensure the ritual is completed, pouring your remaining fortune into the outcome. **Test your Luck.** If successful, turn to **156**. If unsuccessful, turn to **157**.

156

Success! Whether by your final decisive blow, holding the Herald back for the crucial second, or by a burst of fortune guiding the Imam's final words, the ritual is completed!

A blinding column of golden light erupts from Imam Tariq, engulfing the Shaytan's Herald! The creature screams, an unholy sound that shakes the very foundations of the Masjid. The dark energy in the hall is ripped away, drawn into the light. With a final, ear-splitting shriek, the Herald is banished, its form dissolving into nothingness as the light fades.

The oppressive atmosphere lifts instantly. The horrifying presence is gone. Silence falls over the prayer hall, save for your heavy breathing and the sounds of the ongoing, but now faltering, battle outside.

You have done it. You have defeated the Herald and ensured the banishment ritual was completed. Turn to **160**.

157

Failure! Your final effort wasn't enough, or luck was not on your side. You fail to hold the Herald, or your attack is ineffective. The Herald lunges towards Imam Tariq, its eyes burning with triumph, intending to break the ritual at the very last second! The Imam cries out as the Herald's attack slams into him! The ritual is broken!
The Shaytan's Herald laughs, a sound of ultimate victory. The darkness that threatened Asfaran is now unchecked, free to fully manifest. You have failed. The city, and potentially the world, will be plunged into an age of shadow.

Turn to **158**.

158

Your Stamina has reached 0, or your quest has ended in failure. You fought bravely, but the forces against you were too great. The darkness was too much, or a wrong choice led you to ruin. Your adventure ends here. The fate of Asfaran, and perhaps the world, is grim.

Perhaps another hero will take up the mantle and rise to face the darkness.
Start again from the beginning if you wish to try your luck (or skill) again.

Chapter 15: Dawn over the Horizon

The heroes standing together, weary but victorious, looking out over the besieged city from a rooftop. The sun is rising over the horizon, casting light and pushing back the last of the unnatural darkness. The aftermath of the battle – there are damaged buildings, but a sense of peace and relief settling over the scene, conveying hope after hardship.

160

The Grand Masjid is silent. The Shaytan's Herald is gone, banished back to the realms of shadow by the power of the ancient ritual. Dawn is breaking outside, the first rays of sunlight filtering through the high windows of the prayer hall.

Imam Tariq is exhausted but alive, leaning heavily on the Mihrab, his face etched with relief. Your allies – Ali, Jabbar, Zahra – are also weary, covered in dust and likely wounded, but they stand tall, their expressions victorious. The battle outside the Masjid falters. Without the Herald and the Shaytan's direct influence, the corrupted forces are losing cohesion, and the remaining human collaborators or bewildered Crusader allies are being routed by the bolstered defenders. The immediate siege is breaking.

You look out a window, seeing the sunlight washing over the city, pushing back the last vestiges of the unnatural gloom. Asfaran has survived. It is wounded, its people have suffered, but the heart of its faith and its spirit remain unbroken.

You turn back to your companions, the unlikely group brought together by necessity and faith. You have faced immense darkness and prevailed. The Shaytan is banished, for now, the threat to Asfaran averted. But the world outside is still one of conflict, and the realms of shadow are always present.

What will you do now? Your quest to save Asfaran is complete, but your journey as a hero may not be over.

Do you:
- ❖ Choose to stay in Asfaran, to help the city recover, tend to the wounded, and perhaps help Ali organise its defenses against future threats? Turn to **166**.
- ❖ Choose to part ways with your companions for now, seeking new adventures or quests in the wider world, perhaps investigating other areas where the Shaytan's influence was felt? Turn to **167**.
- ❖ Choose to stick with your companions, recognizing the strength of your group and the possibility that other threats, or even the banished Shaytan eventually returning, might require your combined power again? Turn to **168**.

166

You decide to remain in Asfaran. The city needs rebuilding, healing, and strengthening. You dedicate your time and effort to aiding its people, working alongside Ali and Imam Tariq to restore order, comfort the suffering, and reinforce the city's defenses and spiritual strength. Your heroism is remembered and celebrated, and you become a pillar of the community. You find a measure of peace here, having saved the city that first drew you into this conflict.

The End.

167

You bid farewell to your companions, promising that if fate or necessity calls, you will stand together again. Your journey has shown you the depth of the world's perils, but also the potential for heroism. You leave Asfaran, a changed person, ready to face whatever challenges lie in wait across the deserts, mountains, or shadowed lands. A new adventure awaits!

The End.

168

You decide that your bond forged in fire and shadow is too important to break. You agree to remain together as a group, a force for good in a dangerous world. Imam Tariq's knowledge, Jabbar's strength, Ali's leadership, Zahra's stealth, and your own unique abilities are formidable combined. You look to the horizon, knowing that while the Shaytan is banished, darkness ever lurks. Your adventures together are just beginning.

The End.

ABOUT THE AUTHOR

Ashik Usman has a background in Computer Science and Enterprise IT, although before pivoting to the world of technology, he was pursuing Art & Design, and Media Studies. Since the age of 5, he has been an avid fan of fantasy and science fiction, writing stories of his own as a hobby. He enjoys reading, fine arts, cooking authentic and fusion South Asian cuisine. Ashik lives in London with his family.

Printed in Great Britain
by Amazon